Helen Maud Waithman

Charybdis

And other Poems

Helen Maud Waithman

Charybdis
And other Poems

ISBN/EAN: 9783337206888

Printed in Europe, USA, Canada, Australia, Japan

Cover: Foto ©Andreas Hilbeck / pixelio.de

More available books at **www.hansebooks.com**

CHARYBDIS

AND OTHER POEMS

BY

H. M. WAITHMAN

London

EDEN, REMINGTON & CO., PUBLISHERS

KING STREET, COVENT GARDEN

1891

TO MY BELOVED DEAD

No longer earthly homes ye fill ;
   Ye closed your dear eyes peacefully ;
I saw you lying cold and still,
   —Yet ye are here with me.
For Death may close the weary eye,
   And Death may hush the failing breath,
But yours is Immortality
   That triumphs over Death.

CONTENTS

CHARYBDIS

AND OTHER POEMS

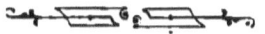

CHARYBDIS

SHE sucketh in men's hearts unto her own ;
    She draws them in like drawing in of breath ;
    Her very life indeed their very death.
She is Charybdis—and they drown ! they drown !

The strongest swimmer has no chance with her ;
    If he but touch the circle of her charm
    In vain he seeks to flee with vague alarm,
Or battles with the strength of doomed despair.

Mad with the lust of conquest and of power
    She blinds him with the rush of blinding sprays,
    She whirls him madly in the whirling maze :
A moment's toy—the triumph of an hour !

Then having worked her will right wilfully,
And he is lifeless, buffeted, undone,
She leaves the haggard corpse to drift alone,
And casts the bleached bones to the sullen sea.

CONSUMMATION

PART I

I SAW your footmark on the sandy track ;
   I followed swift and silent where it led :
So safe you felt you never once looked back
   While Death pursued you with a noiseless tread.

You slipped along betwixt the hedge of yew;
   (As dark and stern it looked as coming fate
To me ; you saw it not—but then I *knew*) ;
   At length you vanished through the wicket gate.

Along the lane,—adown whose rugged banks
   The twisted roots like serpents writhed and spread,
While high above the boughs in serried ranks
   Closed all the day to darkness—on we sped.

We crossed the bridge above the silent stream
   Whose sullen surface never sees the sun ;
So motionless the quiet waters seem
   A leaflet only shows the course they run.

A swooning stillness seemed to hold the air;
   The very voices of the leaves were dumb.
You, who had wrought mine uttermost despair,
   Had had your day—and now my turn was come !

Alone we reached the common.   Still alone
   We fled along beneath the lowering sky.
Meseemed the world a voiceless blank had grown
   Till once I heard a lonely curlew cry.

A lurid streak burned fiercely in the west,
   As red as blood but newly spilt its hue ;
The moorland pool was gashed across the breast
   With its reflection And I thought of you.

I gained upon you swiftly, pace by pace.
   —How sure the feet of Vengeance seem to run !
I neared—I spoke You turned—and saw my face ;
   The steel flashed bravely and the deed was done.

PART II

Then as you lay (O creeping, crimson stain !
  How greedily the grey sand sucked it in !)
I told your deafening ear the tale again
  With all its cruel truths of shame and sin.

I watched your features—but they never stirred ;
  I looked—with every syllable that fell ;
No sign—no sound.   But O ! I pray you heard,
  And took it ringing in your ears to hell.

One thing I *know*—you turned and saw me there,
  And swiftly recognition blanched your cheek.
Though all *I* said but fell on empty air
  You heard your ruined soul's last fearful shriek !

How still you lay.   I could not leave you so.
  Then 'mid the spiny tangle of the gorse
I dragged you.   Well for those who never know
  The strange unsupple weight that makes a corpse.

Now what's for me ! whose days on earth are dead
  To aught of earth save misery and pain,
While Death holds naught but bitterness and dread
  Lest deep in hell I meet you once again.

NEPTUNE'S FLOCKS

VERDANT prairies of the ocean
  Where old Neptune's herds are tended
And his white flocks go a-straying
  Far as ever eye can see ;
Where the dim and utmost distance
  With the sky to one is blended;
Where the way is wild and trackless
  And the wind goes roving free.

On the wide and rolling pastures
  Who shall count the flocks or tend them ?
Does some shepherdess-mermaiden
  Drive them onward through the night ?

Or some Triton, rudely blowing
   On his shell, affrighted send them
Rushing madly in to shoreward
   With their fleeces soft and white ?

We will shear the silver fleeces ;
   We will sit and swiftly spin them
Into cloudy dreams of tissue,
   Such as veil the virgin moon :
We will weave them fine and filmy
   With the dyes of sunset in them,
And will spangle them with star-drops
   Reft from out the nights of June.

Then with deft and dainty touches
   We will delicately shape them
Into hangings rich and splendid
   As no earthly house may hold.
Round life's sordid things and mean ones
   We will softly twine and drape them,
And all rugged edges soften
   'Neath the mystery of their fold.

ERE THAT DAY DAWN

O HEART'S dear heart, will the hours grow dearer
 With the shortening time and the fading light,
While the creeping shadow comes near and nearer
 To end at last in the moonless night?
Shall we grudge each moment that slips away
From the golden hours of our short-lived day?

Shall we say to Love—' We have fast entwined thee?'
 Shall we say to Time—'We would stay thy feet?'
Shall we say to Life—' Were it ours to bind thee
 We would hold thee now, at thy best, complete?'
Shall we smile and say to each other ' Dear,
It is thou art Heaven, and Heaven is here?'

Or shall we say, as the years grow older,

    To Time, ' Make haste, for our hearts are tired ;

Our sun is set, and the hours grow colder,

    And naught is left that can be desired,

For Life is bitter, and Love a lie,

And all we know—It is good to die ! '

Ere that day dawn with its fell disaster

    Let each one pray with an earnest breath,

That the whirl of the chariot-wheels come faster

    That will take us down to the doors of Death ;

For better die while we long to live

Than stay to envy what Death can give.

AVENGED

———

'Yes, you have met your match at last,' said she.
  'You've broken many a heart, and turned away
Sated with "loving." Pah! what blasphemy
  To use *that* word for such an every-day
Occurrence! But you chose to call it so,
  And they—blind foolish women—thought it true.
Poor fools indeed!—but then they did not know
  How mean a thing is "love" to such as you.
Your vanity waxed fat. And then we met.
  You thought to play the self-same game with me.
I watched you walk unconscious to the net
  Yourself had laid so oft and warily!
I drew the meshes closer day by day;
  So slow—but surely. I had time to wait.
I drained your heart's blood drop by drop away,
  You woke at last to face the truth too late.
And here I have you lying at my feet.
  Your heart is breaking, say you? Let it break.
By your own snare brought low! The end is meet.
  And now *you* know how women' hearts can ache.'

A RECKLESS RECORD

———

Come along ! join the whirl and be merry ;
    Let us revel and love and be gay ;
Let us drain the sweet juice of the berry
    As long as we may.

Let us run to the end of our tether
    Regardless of prophecied ban.
What odds ? Let us all go together
    As far as we can.

When the call comes to go we will take you
    As near as we can to the door ;
In farewell by the hand we will shake you.
    What can we do more ?

What matter to us if your pastime
>Has its cost ?   You will have to atone.
We have bid you good-bye for the last time.
>You must face it alone.

We will stay the mad whirl in our sorrow
>For a moment—a day—but no more ;
And the wheel will be turning to-morrow
>As fast as before.

FOILED

He schemed a scheme whereby to make
    Himself beloved ;
He plotted till his heart did ache
    To see it proved.

All day he thought upon the scheme,
    And all the night
It moved before him in his dream
    Till morning's light.

He passed each portion in review
    With anxious care,
To know that every step was true.
    No flaw was there.

He swept all obstacles away
        Without relent,
And crushed whatever might delay
        His full content.

He counted carefully the cost,
        Nor turned afraid
When summing up the uttermost
        The total made.

With silent patience he endured
        The hardest strain ;
Content to wait, so well assured
        The end was gain.

The fruit was ripening in the sun
        To crown the year.
He knew the waiting almost done ;
        The prize was near.

The hour had struck.   Right greedily
        He clutched his gain,
But—Death stepped in, in front of him,
        And all was vain !

A SNOW-STORM

O THE whirling of the snow !
How the flakelets come and go
To and fro, to and fro,
Falling fast, and falling slow
With a shimmer, shimmer, shimmer,
And a glimmer, glimmer, glimmer,
See the world is growing dimmer
In the whirling and dancing of the snow
To and fro.
How the flakelets come and go !
Till one hardly seems to know
Which is heaven, or earth below.
All is dim and undefined
As a dream that haunts the mind.
And the wind—dreary wind !—
Spins and shudders through the blind.
Dream of snow,
Dancing slow,

Whirling wildly to and fro,
Till the earth and sky are set
In a maddening minuet,
Moving softly, treading slow,
Waxing wilder as they go
To and fro, to and fro
In the whirling and the dancing of the snow.
How the flakelets come and go !
With a sudden ebb or flow,
Blown of all the winds that blow
To and fro.
Now they larger seem to grow ;
Falling stately, falling slow ;
Thinking, thinking, as they go
Down to die on earth below,
Full of weariness and woe.
Weirdly wan and weary things ;
Sheeted ghosts on silent wings ;
In a cloud, in a crowd ;
How the wrapping of their shroud
Closely clings !
How the cruel brown earth clutches
Every snow-flake as it touches !

It is dead ere one can tell
Where it fell.   But it fell.
And the others follow faster
To the dolorous disaster
With a fierce and sudden flow ;
Seeking high and seeking low,
    Keen to know.
Finer, finer still they blow
    To and fro, to and fro.
Will they never slack or slow ?
    Never—no !   Never—no !
They will waver to and fro
    Ever more—ever so.
Whirling, whirling, ever whirling
Till the wild white air is swirling
    To and fro, as they go.
And the brain reels to and fro,
    To and fro, to and fro,
With the shimmering silent snow,
With the glamour and the gleaming,
With the drifting and the dreaming,
With the whirling and the dancing of the snow
    To and fro.

WHAT WONDER?

Is it a wonder the wind is grieving
    Out in the passionate world to-day?
Deeds are done that have no retrieving ;
Hearts are hurt that are past relieving ;
    Words are said that we can't unsay.

Is it a wonder the clouds are flying
    Over the pitiless world to-day?
Voices call that have no replying ;
Ears are closed to the sound of crying ;
    Hearts are hardened and turned away.

Is it a wonder the rain is falling
    Over the sorrowful world to-day?
Links are broken once all-enthralling ;
Bonds are tightened and chains are galling,
    —Freed or fettered, alike dismay !

Wail, oh wind, with a plaintive wailing !

    Pain and Passion grow rank and rife.

Fly, oh clouds, from the woes prevailing !

Weep, oh rain, with a fount unfailing !

    Endless ills are the ills of life.

THE SONG OF THE LARK

An Angel came to the Earth one day
  On a Mission sent, and he felt forlorn
So far in the desolate world away;
  So he sat him down in the rustling corn,
And with heart aweary and folded wing
He sang the song he was used to sing.

Then all things listened to hear the song
  As it throbbed, and swelled, and was upward borne ;
In the heart of the breeze it was swept along
  And he whispered it down to the ears of corn,
Who bowed their heads as his voice went by
And told each other the melody.

The slumbering poppy the sound o'erheard ;
  She brake in haste in her downy shell
And spread her petals to hold each word.

And when the shade of the evening fell
In the daisy's heart and the buttercup
The song of the angel was folded up.

A squirrel sat on a bough near by
    Like a carven squirrel ; and every bird
Had hushed, and was listening silently;
    And never a leaf of the woodland stirred.
E'en the shy mice crept through the stalks of wheat
And nestled close to the singer's feet.

The sound was hushed, and the song was done;
    The angel passed from the field away,
And never a creature that heard, save one,
    Could quite remember the tender lay.
They strove their best, and some notes were theirs;
But the lark knew all, and the song was hers.

So that is why as she sings she soars,
    For the song within her will seek its home,
And it bears her up to the golden doors
    Till it hears the echoing answer come;
Then filled with patience it sinks to rest
Content to wait in the lark's grey breast.

STAR DAISIES

Hearts of gold that the white rims hold,
  Like amber wine in a silver chalice !
Stars that slipped through the frosty night
Down the sky, and were hid from sight
Deep in earth, that at last they might
  Blossom as flowers in the Summer's palace.

Daylight dims, and a soft wind skims,
  With wings as light as the night-moth's hover.
White and weird is the daisies' dance ;
Weird and strange as an old romance.
Ghosts of stars that awake from trance
  Call to the stars that are shining over :

' Stars so high in the midnight sky !
  Sweet sister stars in the purple setting !
Wrapped in robes that are silver cold

Yet warm our hearts as in days of old,
—Robes of silver, but hearts of gold ;
   Fallen from heaven, but unforgetting.

'Do ye know we are here below ?
   Man's heart looked up to the distant shining ;
Far were we in the utmost blue;
Vain his yearning—ah ! well we knew—
So we fell to the earth and grew
   Answer sweet to his soul's repining.

'Is the cost of our labours lost ?
   Nay, sister-stars, it hath full repaying.
Earth is glad where we bloom and blow ;
Man's heart sings when he sees us grow.
Love is ours in the world below.
   Heaven is ours after Love's delaying.'

Daisies fade in the sun and shade ;
   Fair petals fall as the year is flying,
But each daisy that blooms and dies
Shines once more in the midnight skies.
Silver robes were a fair disguise
   But hearts of gold are as stars undying.

THE COURSE OF TIME

THE course of Time counts not by days or years,
But measures long or short by joy or tears ;
Joy, all absorbed, marks not his rapid flight,
Years pass unheeded as a summer's night ;
But sorrow binds his wings—he creeps away—
An age of anguish centred in a day.

AN OLD-FASHIONED CONCEIT

LONG lashes, like tall rushes, fringe the brink
    Of those two limpid lakes—my true love's eyes ?
Love leaned o'er them from their sweet depths to drink
    And still he mirrored on their surface lies.

THE BALLAD OF FORRABURY BELLS

———

HARK ! do you hear them ?   How the bells are tolling,
　　　Across the bay to-night ?
Amid the roar and crash of billows rolling
　　　With furious might,
Higher than wind or wave in music, swells
The loud mysterious tolling of the bells.

How came they there ?—Have you not heard the story ?
　　　Then listen while I tell
How they are chanting—' To the Lord the Glory ! '
　　　And every bell
Sings the same strain, and joins with sweet accord
In bidding all who hear them—' Praise the Lord ! '

Long years ago the folk of Forrabury
　　　Resolved to have a chime,

To gaily ring when folk were blithe and merry,
  Or toll at time
Of death ; for hitherto, as you must know,
No bells had waked the silence of Bottreaux.

And so the bells were ordered ; and the casting
  Completed, they were blessed.
Then safe on shipboard, soon were swiftly hasting
  To their last rest.
So fair a voyage on so calm a sea
Along that coast was never known to be.

But while they waited for the tide's inflowing,
  To cross the harbour-bar,
Across the downs Tintagel's bells were throwing
  Their music far.
The pilot heard the vesper chime, and said :—
'Thanks be to God, Whose Hand hath safely led.'

Then long the Captain laughed, while loudly swearing
  No other thanks were due
Than to the noble ship, his anxious caring,
  The trusty crew.
He scorned the pilot's praying, and he swore
Sans God, *himself* to bring them safe ashore.

' May God forgive you!' said the pilot sadly ;
   And even as he spoke
The great Atlantic wave sped swiftly, madly.
    It swelled—and broke !*
Where now was gallant ship or trusty crew ?
Gone—like the glitter of the morning dew.

Gone, deep beneath the waste of furious ocean ;
    No more to re-appear.
High on the cliffs in terror and emotion
    They huddled near
Who had been watching till the ship should ride
Safe into harbour with the coming tide.

Only the pilot landed, safely clinging
    To some light-floating spar.
The bells were lost forever ; but their ringing
    Is heard afar
Sounding the voice of warning o'er the deep
When wild winds rage and angry billows leap.

---

 * 'Those who are familiar with the northern shores of Cornwall will know that sometimes a huge wave, generated by some mysterious power in the wide Atlantic will roll on, overpowering everything with its weight.'

Silence still broods in Forrabury Tower ;
    No bells are swinging there
For joy or grief, or yet to call the hour
    Of praise and prayer.
But from the sea, that men may not forget,
'To God the praise ! ' the bells are chiming yet.

A L O N E

————..

Alone, alone, forevermore alone.

    The others pass her by

    With laughing eye,

    With voices ringing cheerily

    And answering so merrily;

    Hands clasped in hands,

    Face turned to face.

    And here she stands

Alone, alone, alone, in her own place.

Alone, alone, forevermore alone.

    And yet she hath not heart of stone.

    Perchance that Galatea-wise

    She looks a statue to their eyes.

'Tis only in her loneliness alone
She maketh moan,
And wringeth empty hands,
And waveth empty arms unto the sky,
And cries with an exceeding bitter cry
That no one understands.

Alone, alone, forevermore alone.
    They say—she is so cold;
    Who would be over-bold
To call her from those icy summits down?
    Who would disturb the wise
    Sad slumber of her eyes,
Lest looking graver still she also frown?

Alone, alone, forevermore alone.
    They say—oh let her be!
    She lives so dreamily;
She has no part with us nor we with her.
    We will no sad-faced ghost,
    We will no voiceless image mute,
To throw a shadow 'mid the merry host,
To chill the sound of laughter and of lute.
There where she stands so still we leave her there.

Alone, alone, forevermore alone.

And so they passing reck no more of her.

> They pass her by so cheerily,
>
> With voices ringing merrily;
>
> Hands clasped in hands,
>
> Face turned to face.
>
> And there she stands

Stone-cold and tearless in her dumb despair.

Alone, alone, forevermore alone.

> Never a hand to clasp *her* soft and warm,
>
> Never an arm to shield *her* from the storm,

Never a voice to say to her ' My own ! '

> Ah no ! unto herself she must suffice;
>
> Be her own altar, her own sacrifice;
>
> Grow used to watch the Future all alone;
>
> Blink back the unshed tears that sometimes start
>
> And drop them slowly, slowly, on her heart;
>
> Bind to her side her arms lest their appeal
>
> Should show the world the emptiness they feel;
>
> Guard her slow tongue, keep watch upon her eyes,
>
> That all may think—O dreariest of lies !

That she is quite content to be alone.

Alone, alone, forevermore alone.

' Behold ! ' they say—' this miracle of stone !

This self-sufficing dreamer ! *Living*—still

    So unresponsive, self-contained and chill.

    She would not condescend to such as we,

    And so we do not love her.' Meanwhile she

    Listens with ears that hear—with heart that cries,

    Speechless, expressionless, save in her eyes

    A slow smile creeps, a smile as sad as death,

    For she, who sees the surface underneath,

    Watches the throes and hears the parting sighs

Of one lone soul—and no one knows it dies.

EDGED TOOLS

———

Ah, sure 'tis ill to play with edged tools,
  To trifle with a dagger 'just for fun,'
And show the silly bravery of fools
  Who misappreciate the risk they run.

Come, pretty fool, and have a game of play !
  I'll make the little bauble spark and shine,
And turn it this and that and every way;
  Only, the handle I must hold as mine.

Just the plain handle; *that* was never made
  For dainty fingers, slim and fair as those.
See the fine glitter of the polished blade.
  How the reflected fire-light burns and glows.

(·

Mark how the steel is deftly damascened
  With quaint device and delicate design;
How through the moonlit blue wherewith 'tis sheened,
  The gold and silver fancies intertwine.

See at each gentlest moving of the wrist,
  How the blade flashes!   By some magic spell
It seems as if at every turn and twist
  A shower of diamond arrows fled and fell.

Ha! fool! hast slipped? and has it pierced thy heart,
  And brought the life-blood welling through the wound?
Ah well, the fault's not mine; I played my part
  To please thee—and my hand is whole and sound.

RE-ARISEN

I HID it away in a deep dark closet
  In the house of my heart ; and I locked the door
And wrote on the threshold :—' Behold ! this was it-
  The love that I bore, but I bear no more.'

I hung fair wreaths at the dreary portal,
  Sweet flowers that blossom, frail flowers that fade,
For I said—' As are they, so my love is mortal ;
  Though it bloomed in the sun it will die in the shade.'

Then was silence. But when 'twas broken
  By the thin keen sound of the coldest word
That ever the lips of a friend have spoken
  The love that was hidden awoke and stirred.

Awoke and stirred, and arose and thundered
   At the door that was closed till it brake it through
And stood in the light ; and my faint heart wondered,
   For I thought it had *died*—and behold it *grew !*

As its strong feet trod on the faded wreathings
   Their scent rose sweet on the troubled air,
And the sere leaves told by their balmy breathings
   That the soul of the roses still lingered there.

It were vain to hide it again—the sorrow
   Of the sweet lost love and the sad sharp pain,
For at sound of a voice if it spoke to-morrow,
   It would break from the deeps of its tomb again.

So I let it stand where I needs must see it
   —Like the dead man guest at an old time feast—
Till at last no more shall I seek to flee it
   When my old wild dread of its power has ceased.

A MYTH-MAIDEN

———

SOMEWHERE in story they found her;

    In a myth-robe grey

    She was hidden away

With the mists of the morning round her.

Then they dragged her forth to the light of day,

And decked her all in a garment gay,

    And with wreaths of fancies crowned her.

But the ghosts that loved her in days long dead

Know her not with her crownèd head,

    And her robes of silver and golden thread.

They mourn the robe that she wore erewhile;

The faint soft flush, and the fair sweet smile;

    The life retiring, and free from guile.

They mourn and will not be comforted.

For who would know that the garish dame,

With the bold bright eyes and the lips of flame

And the doubtful praise of a well-known name,

  Could be the same

   As the pale sweet may

   In the myth-robe grey

  With the mists of the morning round her.

YE ARE DUMB DOGS

'Dumb dogs' are we.   Ay me, but it is so.
　　Who does not know the untold agony
Of his own dumbness? and the speechless woe
　　Of seeming that which he the least would be?

I, who would pour my very soul to you
　　In one wild flood of passionate appeal,
Or in a language eloquent and true
　　My best, most real self, would fain reveal,

Am dumb!—Ah dumb!—I speak—my lips belie
　　My heart's best meanings, make them poor and cold;
Or masquerade them, set them all awry,
　　Till it were best they had been quite untold.

Or,—surging with the silent storm within,—
  With passionless conventionality
I sit and talk of this and that; the din
  Of outer voices drowns the inner cry.

Words! What are words? A mask, a shield whereby
  We hide ourselves, lest others know too well
That we would keep, or they perchance should spy
  The hidden things we break our hearts to tell!

So, overflowed as with a torrent's might
  With all the day has prisoned dumb and dead,
I spend the silent watches of the night
  In saying all my lips must leave unsaid.

Fired with an eloquence unknown by day,
  Filled with a candour born of stilly night,
My heart her wonted barriers tears away
  And empties all her thoughts in freed delight;

And joying, to herself she gaily tells :—
  'This will I *say*.' When will to-morrow come?'
The morning breaks, renewing daylight's spells;
  —We meet—and lo! my heart again is dumb.

REST

'Oh that I had the wings of a dove! Then would I fly away
and be at rest.'

———

WOULD you do so, my heart? Would you do so?
Where would you go?
Where is there rest for you on land or sea?
On what fair branches of what tall green tree
'Mid leaves that sigh and whisper in the wind
Rest would you find?

There is no rest, my heart, for you—no rest,
No place to nest.
What though with wearied wings you strive to fly
Ten million miles beneath the heedless sky
To seek it—Though you fly till night shall fall,
—No rest at all.

There is no rest, my heart, for you, because
                    Unspoken laws
Say surely that the heart who rest would know
Must take it with him.   If he do not so
He will not find it anywhere.   Is rest
                    Within your breast?

And so 'tis wise, oh heart, to sit and wait
                    The ways of Fate;
Not spend your energies in useless flight
But hoard them for the fresh on-coming fight.
Patience will bring her sister Rest anon
                    If you wait on.

TOGETHER

———

OLD Father Time knew a youth and knew a maiden,
 And he watched them older growing,
 As the years were onward going
With fair youth and pleasure laden.
Old Father Time knew they were for one another,
 So he guided all their paces
 Far away from distant places
Till they met and loved each other.

Old Father Time laid his hand on them, caressing,
 Saying :—' Love so well and dearly,
 That I, at my coming yearly,
May but bring a richer blessing.'

Old Father Time saw them on life's journey moving,
    Watched them as they went together
    Through the fair and stormy weather
Ever more devoted proving.

Old Father Time came at last unto them saying :—
    ' Ye must leave me for my brother;
    God hath said it and no other;
Ye must go without delaying.'
' Dear Father Time,' said they, ' we have ne'er been parted ! '
    So they passed out hand in hand
    Out into the Silent Land,
To the land of the true-hearted.

ALTERNATIONS

To-day I have a voice that sings
    Like a wee bird within my heart;
My spirits fly on joyful wings;
    No longer life hath teen or smart;
        Its stings
        Depart.

To-morrow finds me sad, distressed,
    Bowed down with burden of my woe;
So sorrow-laden and opprest,
    As if my weary heart could know
        No rest
        Below.

To-day it is a joy to be;
　To see the children of the spring
Upbreak in blossom gloriously,
　And all things to her welcoming
　　　Agree
　　　To sing.

To-morrow—ah ! the day is long.
　If years be made of days like this
One needs to ' suffer and be strong ! '
　To days that are so much amiss
　　　Belong
　　　No bliss.

To-day Hope sits beside my hand,
　And tells me tales of by-and-bye ;
Fair tales I fain would understand,
　Yet am content to wait till I
　　　Shall stand
　　　Anigh.

To-morrow leaden-hued Despair
　Blots all things other out of sight ;
Makes every trivial grief a care,

And saps the heart from out delight
　　With her
　　Keen blight.

To-day a sunbeam radiance throws
　　That lights to gold the meanest things.
With light and warmth divine it glows;
　　The frozen heart anew upsprings
　　　　And grows
　　　　And sings.

To-morrow clouds obscure the sun,
　　And drown his golden rays in rain;
The shadows grow, and one by one
　　The happy sparkling lights are slain
　　　　Till none
　　　　Remain.

Thus now with fairest blooms of May,
　　Anon with winter snows besprent
Life passes.　Thus enveiled in grey
　　Or with fulfilment of content
　　　　Each day
　　　　Is spent.

WORLD'S DAWNING

WE strive to find the Dawn. We peer
Adown the utmost Past, and say
' Behold the Dawning ! it was here ! '
　But as it grows more clear and clear
The fragments of an older day
Behind this dawning reappear.

Yet far and farther on we go.
　From dawn to dawn we slowly track,
As following ever further back
　Our age-long days in numbers grow,
And yet another day we lack,
　Another dawning's earliest glow !

Where is the Dawning? Where, oh! where?
  Like peevish babes we cry to see.
Why vex thy soul, oh man? or care
  So much to know?—lest thou despair;
For Past alike with Yet-to-be
  Is circled by Eternity.

A G E

———

WHY is the face of age unbeautiful,
                Worn, faded, dull?
The limbs so feeble, back so lowly bent,
                The strength all spent?
The thought of Present, Past and Future sprinkles
                The brow with wrinkles.
The constant wear and fret of daily cares
                Brings forth grey hairs.
Tears wrung from out the heart's deep agonies
                Bedim the eyes.
The weight of this world's heavy-loaded pack
                Bows down the back.
The endless struggling will produce at length
                The lack of strength.

The feeble feet are tired with having trod
        The road to God.
But scorn not age, for 'neath its homely face
        Oft canst thou trace
The hidden angel who stands waiting there
        Divinely fair.

AT VARIANCE

HIMSELF-that-is, Himself-that-fain-would-be
Are wakened to a war of enmity;
 And he is torn with agony of strife,
 With keen upbraidings, sharper than a knife
 That cut into the very core of life.

His would-be self, unbending, stern, erect,
Proud with the pride that springs from self-respect;
 Armed with a love of truth defined and strong;
 Seeking the Right, intolerant of wrong;
 Ready to battle, and to battle long.

Himself-that-is, weak, passionate and vain,
Of love and admiration over-fain;
 Moved by false sentiment to sympathy;

Soothing itself with specious sophistry,
Eager to gain its ends in peace thereby.

Thus stand they; and his soul is battle-field,
One must be victor; one must surely yield.
Fearful and unrelenting is the fight
Thro' the long day, and thro' the longer night.
Which will be victor?—God defend the right!

SONNET

IT is not when we *part* that we should weep,
　　But when we *meet* that we must part again.
　　I almost deem it is the keener pain
That thro' our happy hours sad thoughts should creep;
Like some grey dream that haunts our quiet sleep,
　　The which we hate and hide from,—but in vain.
　　Thro' all our songs of welcome the refrain
' We meet to part '—re-echoes stern and deep.

But when we part we say : ' If God shall will
We'll meet again.　Speed, Time, with flying feet.'
　　And should we meet no more then let us still
Content us to abide till we shall meet
　　Beyond terrestrial power of good or ill,
Where all unfinished joys are made complete.

'GOD KNOWS'

After a wreck off Dungeness the body of a baby was washed ashore ;
it was buried with the above epitaph.

_____

' GOD knows.'   Oh little babe so quiet sleeping
   Enfolded on the kind Earth-Mother's breast,
No fond hearts bend above thee, sadly weeping,
   No sound of grief disturbs thy perfect rest.

None deck thy little grave because they love thee,
   But God's sun shines o'er it, God's daisy grows,
And God's green grass waves tenderly above thee,
   For nothing is forgotten that ' God knows.'

We have no name for thee ; but up in glory
   Where baby-angels see His face—of those
Thou art the playmate, and they know thy story
   And call thee by the hidden name God knows.

Thy Mother has not lost thee, little baby ;

When she awakes at last from her repose

She'll cry ' Where is my child ! '—and then—ah may be

God's voice will say—' Here is thy child. God knows.'

AN OLD-MAID'S STORY

YES, I too had my day.   Some two or three
Kind friends would also gladly lovers be,
But love and lovers had no charm for me.

Ah yes, no doubt that they were good and kind,
All that a maid may hope or wish to find.
But some there are whom Love leaves deaf and blind.

For me—the circle of my life was set
About a deep and infinite regret.
And through all haps it is life's centre yet.

All have their stories somewhere hidden deep;
With some perchance they slumber—Let them sleep—
While some still wake and watch and inly weep.

'LOVE'S YOUNG DREAM'

I saw them standing in a wood,
   Just where the light fell strong and clear;
I peeped--I don't suppose I should—
   They did not know that I was near.

It was a morning in the Spring;
   The world was gay; the sun was bright,
And all the little birds that sing
   Were telling of their heart's delight.

And just where larchen-branches hide
   The path from view of this their nook,
Those two were standing, side by side,
   And near them ran a tinkling brook.

I knew 'twas Love's spring holiday
    For they most certainly were dressed
In garments very fresh and gay;
    —I noticed his canary vest.

I could not hear the words they said,
    But they were talking, it was plain,
For now and then he bobbed his head,
    And then she nodded back again.

And once or twice I saw them kiss!
    They did!—This tale is strictly true.
But, then, you know, that's not amiss,
    'Tis just what other lovers do.

The brooklet laughed as it ran by,
    The sunlight touched them here and there;
It made his vest like summer shine,
    And lighted up her golden hair.

They were so sweet, unconscious, fair,
    —The memory still my bosom thrills,—
And long I stood and watched them there
    That pretty pair of *daffodils*.

HASTE!

LITTLE bird with a song in your heart,
    Sing, oh sing,
Ere the hours of the sunshine depart,
And night cometh—the desolate thing.

Little bud that looks up to the sun
    Haste to blow
Ere the race of the summer be run;
Winter cometh with wrappings of snow.

Little heart that is young, O be glad
    While you may,
Ere you sigh for the youth that you had;
For age cometh, and death, and decay.

D A W N

THE pale dawn-maiden stands upon the hill,
  And gazes o'er the land
That sleeping lies so very calm and still
Yet seems with rapture of her gaze to thrill.
  She raises up her hand,
And with her rosy fingers shades her eyes
So soft and full of dream-like mysteries
  That few can understand.

She stands so still, no wonder that the hush
  Grows more and more profound.
Then suddenly a fair and dainty flush
Creeps o'er her face; it deepens to a blush;
  The awakening earth turns round
A sleepy shoulder, and the ambushed sun
Springs forth to find her. Lo! he findeth none!
  She has fled without a sound.

BEGGAR'S SONG TO THE WIND

———

Howl, dreary wind, and beat about the house;
 I love to hear thy melancholy crying.
   I, too, as thou, am free
   To beat my misery
On doors and windows closed against my sighing.

Wind, had'st thou been the rich and balmy breath
 That summer lades with her divinest essence,
   Then, doors and windows wide
   To let thee come inside,
Had each man craved the honour of thy presence.

None, thou must know, but he who somewhat brings
 Of joy or wealth, is welcome in appearing;
   But be he sick or sad,
   Or poor, or meanly clad,
Eyes see him not, and ears grow hard of hearing.

S O N G

———

Love can live on so little !
  He does not ask much;
A look or a whisper,
  A smile or a touch.
      Love can live on so little.

Love can live on so little !
  Yet if there be more
How gladly he grasps it
  To add to his store.
      Love can live on so little.

Love can live on so little !
  If that you deny

He painfully pining
And starving, must die.
　　　　Love can live on so little.

Love can live on so little !
Ah will you not give
That little ungrudging
That still he may live?
　　　　Love can live on so little.

TRIFLING

'I say I do not care, and yet
   I find my heart sings songs of glee
That we may meet or we have met.'
  'Who?' 'Well, you see
If I perchance should tell you who
   Then you would know! so that would be
   A thing I hardly care to do.'
  'Why?' 'You'll agree
There are some things 'tis better far
   Are only known to *two*—not *three;*
So if I told you who *we* are—'
  'Who?'—'*I* am *She!*
But then you knew that well before,
   Of course you say disgustedly.

E

You'd like to know a little more ? '

' Yes, who—'   ' Is *He ?*

What ! would you really like to know ?

A vital question !—who are *we ?*

I'll tell you—let the grammar go—'

' Well—'   ' *Him* and *Me !*

Ah ! now you're getting vexed a bit !

D'you think I care ?—Perhaps I do.

So listen, while I whisper it—

We're—I and *You !* '

THE VALLEY OF LOST SUNSETS

BEHIND the misty ridge of blue
   The suns of all the yesterdays
Fill all the valley hid from view
   With one transcendent golden blaze.
What other treasures harbour here,
   —Lost treasures that the Past have blest ?
Perchance 'the snows of yester-year,'
   The birds that flew from last year's nest.

There where the gilded light is fed
   With suns of all the yesterdays,
The roses of lost summers shed
   Their scented petals o'er the ways,

'Mid sounds of all the brooks that purled,
　　And whispering trees and songs of birds;
—Lost myriad voices that the world
　　Makes music to the heart's own words.

Here, too, their beauty re-illumed
　　By suns of all the yesterdays,
Our lost illusions lie entombed
　　In shimmering veils of sunset haze.
Those glints of heaven that with us stayed
　　When thence to earth we newly stepped,
But doomed—ah me !—to fail and fade
　　As slowly on through life we crept.

Here, dallying in the golden beams
　　Of suns of all the yesterdays,
Are dreams that once were only dreams,
　　And hopes fulfilled without delays.
Here life's lost morning breaks once more
　　With bloom of lovely youth eterne.
And Time from out its garnered store
　　Lets all our wasted hours return.

And here, maybe, we'll find erewhile
    With suns of all the yesterdays,
Lost voices speak, lost faces smile,
    Lost eyes look back our loving gaze.
Old loves will live, old hurts be healed,
    Old ills forgot in new-found good;
And in that glorious light revealed
    Old errors will be understood.

Farewell, oh sun that joins to-night
    The suns of all the yesterdays,
Merging your solitary light
    In their entirety. The days
Are shortening now; when done they be
    I'll climb the ridge—that lies so far
I cannot reach it now—and see
    The Valley where lost sunsets are.

'NOW IS THE WINTER OF OUR DISCONTENT'

THE sighs of the whole world sigh in the wind,
  The moans of the whole world moan in the trees.
  Our hearts are weary and ill at ease,
  Our minds are dreary and hard to please:
And looking and listening, what is to find?
          — Nothing but these.

For the wind is the woe of the world gone by;
  The sad soft sighings that have been sighed,
  Grown and gathered from every side
  And sweeping by in a swelling tide,
Till beating and breaking, the piteous cry
          Flieth awide.

And the trees are attuned to a bygone moan;
  The moans of many all mingled there,

Wrought and wrung from the hearts of care,
Till the branches pulse to the great despair,
And wracking and wringing, the gaunt arms groan,
Beating the air.

The world is grey with the damp of tears;
Rain of tears that have long been shed,
Drawn from the wells of the eyes long dead
Up through the grass and the mouldy bed,
And filt'ring and falling through all the years,
Fed and re-fed.

And where is laughter? and where is love?
Born and buried with sweet flowers blown;
Wafted away with the thistle-down;
Fleeted and fled when the birds are flown;
Buried beneath us, or vanished above;
Left us—alone.

And now is the winter. Our discontent
Grows great and greater as days go by;
We add to the sob of the wind a sigh,
We add to the moan of the trees a cry,
In the age-long sound of the world's lament
Never to die!

HAYMAKING

SWEET June roses were all ablow,
Scythes swung steadily to and fro,
Ripe grass fell in a level row,
      Oh happy days!—Heigh ho!

Strong arms tossing the dying grass,
Raking, lading, and carts that pass;
Song and sunshine, and lad and lass.
      Oh happy days!—Heigh ho!

Light hearts laughed with the day begun;
Laughed at noon with the laughing sun;
Laughing still when the day was done.
      Oh happy days!—Heigh ho!

Days of happiness! Hours of play!
Time has carted you all away;
Stored you by, like the scented hay.
      Oh happy days! Heigh ho!

LEAFY TOWN

THE year is young, and the world is gay;
  The sun shines out with a golden sheen;
The sweet birds twitter and sing all day;
  And endless delicate shades of green
Are creeping over the woodland brown,
For life is waking in Leafy-Town.

Then roses open, and days grow long.
  The lazy breezes that wander by
Go whispering ever the leaves among
  The 'latest news' of the sea and sky;
And each tree rustles her dainty gown,
For now is 'the Season' in Leafy-Town.

The corn is carried; the daylight wanes;
    The stripling breeze to a wind is grown;
There is hardly a rose on the bush remains;
    The Summer's birds to the South are flown.
And scarlet, crimson, and shades of brown
Are now 'the fashion' in Leafy-Town.

The year is old, and the days grow chill;
    The rain is heavy, the skies are grey;
The frost is sharp, and the wind is shrill
    And blows in pitiless blasts all day.
Then shuddering, sadly, the leaves fall down,
And life is over in Leafy-Town.

SONGS

As we sit in the midst of the time that is To-day
We hear the pipers piping and the children at their play,
And the merry youths and maidens as they dance are
     singing gay.
And we listen to their song till we sighing turn away;
Then we look, smiling—sighing, in each other's eyes and
     say :—
'There is never Now a song like the songs of Yesterday!'

So we listen, sitting still, with a smile and with a sigh.
Is the piping getting fainter?　Are the children all
     gone by ?
Are the singers growing weary, for the voices fail and die ?
Or is our hearing failing ?—Are we failing—you and I ?—
Then we look with a smile in each other's eyes, and cry,
'There is never Now a song like the songs of By-and-By.'

SUPPOSING

THEY met beneath a tree, and lingered talking;
  Her eyes were very bright and clear and blue.—
He said ' Supposing we continue walking,
  For I should like so much to walk with you.'
She answered with a blush and softly smiling :—
  ' Supposing—yes—supposing that we do.'

He said :—' If I should tell you that I love you;
  Have loved you long, and tenderly, and true.
Supposing—I am only just supposing—
  That you for answer said, " I love you too ! " '
The answer slipped quite softly through the twilight
  ' Supposing—oh !—supposing that I do !'

He said :—' If I should ask you for a kiss, dear,
  And were not quite content with one, or two !
I wonder will you take it much amiss, dear,
  Supposing, pretty sweetheart, that I do !'
The answer crept like echo of a whisper,
  ' Supposing ah ! supposing that you do !'

OUR PLAY

So now, farewell! our little play is over,
    The curtain falls at last,
And our twain parts as loved one and as lover
        Are of the past.

As we rehearsed our rôles with care unending,
    For weeks, the live-long day,
No wonder there was such success attending
        Our little play.

The plot was full of scene and situation
    That strengthened as they passed,
Until the changing, sudden consummation
        Of Act the Last.

'A marriage,' said the lookers on, deluded,
  'Will end the whole affair ;'
They did not know 'a comedy' concluded
        With some despair.

The scene—a country house.   What more was needed
  Than garden, roses, trees?
A terrace, too?   Oh, many a play succeeded
        With less than these.

We played our parts full well.   I call attention
  To points—just two or three—
So like to life, it were as well to mention
        Their *un*reality.

That scene   you know—the one where you were sitting
  Just where the moonlight fell;
And I, your lover, took,—as was but fitting,
        My cue so well.

Ah! 'twas well done!   My voice was full of passion,
  My words were fire!   In sooth,
So like to truth— but then, 'tis not the fashion
        To speak the truth.

And you had face suffused with rosy flushes;
  The moon lit up your eyes.
Not all who act can thus command their blushes
      And find them rise.

Your eyes, your voice were all 'neath your controlling,
  So perfect was your art;
Your very heart and soul as aids enrolling,
      You *lived* the part.

Have you forgot that scene too 'neath the willow
  Whose branches hung so low?
Your head had claimed my shoulder as its pillow,
      —Nay—do not go!—

And I was whispering words of adoration
  Close to that pretty ear.
'Twas life-like quite. I know my intonation
      Was true and clear.

And oft we kissed. Ah heaven! if *acted* kisses
  Are sweet and mad as those,
How sweet, how mad, how rapturous his bliss is
      Who *really* knows.

Shall I go on?   The scenes were very many,
    But *I* remember well.
Have *you* forgotten one—or all—or any
         That I could tell?

Nay do not say this is recrimination,
    'Tis idle chat—no more.
Friends like to talk, with fond re-iteration,
         The old times o'er.

I have not ended quite.   The tale is thrilling
    Here, nearing to the end;
It were but just to praise your grand fulfilling
         Your part, my *friend*.

Oh that last Act!   My blind infatuation,
    —Brought to so swift an end.
My maddened burst of wrath and desperation
         —Could that be penned?

Your coolness—my mad passion—your betraying—
    My broken hearted grief,
Your tone sarcastic—Oh 'twas wondrous playing!
         Beyond belief!

To you be all the credit.   'Twas your doing,
   The comedy begun
Turned to a tragedy, with endless rueing,
      The part of one.

An actor's life they say is worn with tension
   Of constant nervous strain.
And *now* I know that is no mere invention
      To pity gain.

Indeed the strain is sharp beyond all knowing
   And very hard to bear !
Since then my face is lined, and grey is shewing
      Upon my hair.

I must not let you go till I have given
   Thanks for the lesson learned.
The fee seems great; but you so well have striven
      'Tis justly earned.

F

B U T—

———.

HE played with a broken old lantern
  In the gutter, down there in the street:
His face was all streaky and grimy,
  But his eyes were so sweet.
He spoke, and his patois was horrid,
  But his accents were mild;
He was dirty and lived in the gutter,
  But he was a child.

A FANCY

You are part of a previous life,
  I have met you I know not where,
But I was your promised wife,
  And you were my lover there.

I remember the way you wooed,
  And the look in your eyes the while.
I know every passing mood,
  And the curve of the coming smile.

And your step as you cross the floor,
  With a manly and even tread,
Is the step that I heard of yore,
  In the days ere we both were dead.

You have changed not a whit since then
  In aught but one trifling thing,
—That you were my king of men,
  And now you are not my king.

A WOMAN

A woman with a story. Such
  Are many. Aye, the world is sad
And sorry; sometimes overmuch
  We seem to miss the good and glad.

A woman with a story. See
  Its lines are written on her face.
So sad and weary-eyed is she
  That life and she seem out of place.

Her story? Woman's usual role
  Of worshipping a worthless clod;
She cast the mantle of her soul
  About a man, and deemed him god.

And when, as length of days wore on,
　Her god's false godship fell away
Until at length 'twas wholly gone,
　She broke her heart to find him clay.

She has not murmured or complained;
　To such as she all words are vain.
Some souls there are, who deadly-pained
　Grow dumb, and never speak again.

So closèd-lipped and weary-eyed,
　Her constant sorrow with her stays;
From all the world they stand aside;
　And thus within her soul she prays :—

' God ! shut this page down of my book,
　And seal it close, and keep it sealed
That none may on its story look
　Till every secret stand revealed ! '

A BONFIRE

It's true. I *am* engaged, old boy,
    And as we are the best of friends,
Come home with me while I destroy
    Some ' relics '—just some odds and ends.
Ah here's a jolly fire ablaze.
    And this you'll find a good cigar,
While I discourse of ancient days
    And show you what these ' relics ' are.

This drawer is full. I keep it locked.
    —You have one just the same no doubt—
If Someone saw she might be shocked ;
    'Tis best for both to clear it out.

You see this twist of gilded cord—
   One gave me that from off her fan.
Her great ambition was a lord,
   And I was but a gentleman !

And here are half-a-dozen gloves,
   —All odd ones, as you may suppose—
The gifts of half-a-dozen loves.
   —Who were they ?—Well *now* goodness knows !
Some flowers all withered brown and dry,
   With nothing left of form or scent,
A pack of photographs. Good-bye !
   My pretty friends ! 'Tis time ye went.

I had this little silver ring
   From one dear friend I used to know.
She died. 'Tis but a paltry thing,
   But still I will not let that go.
This box is filled with locks of hair,
   Of every shade, I think, but grey !
What touching scenes are figured there,
   And *now*—their owners who were they ?

No, this affair's not *all* romance;
  It has enough of common sense
To give poor mortals just a chance
  Of happiness without pretence.
Be my 'best man,' old fellow.   *Do!*
  You've been my kindest friend thro' life;
You must be friends with Edith too,
  I know that you will like my wife.

CARPE DIEM!

I AM filling my own cup
  Full of poison to the brim,
And I needs must drain it up
  Though the end be dire and grim.
Let me drink ! let me drink !
  For the poison drops are sweet;
And I will not stay to think
  For the moments are so fleet.
It is sweet ! it is strong,
  And the tumult of my soul
In a flood-tide flows along,
  Mad, and reckless of control.
It is strong, it is grand !
  And it makes life doubly good;
So I cannot stay my hand,
  —And I would not if I could !

This is nectar for the gods !
Tell me nought of by-and-bye
And its anguish ; what's the odds !
Let me drain it though I die.
Every drop as it drops
Is new life in death to me;
When the power to pour it stops
So will I.   Let me be !
I will drink it and be glad;
Life is only short at best;
Grasp the pleasure to be had,
And a murrain take the rest !
Let me drink !   Let me drink !
For the poison drops are sweet;
And I will not stay to think,
For the moments are so fleet.
Not an hour left to waste !
Life is precious, every breath;
And I would not lose a taste,
For this is a race with Death.
Fill the cup ! fill it up !
For the time is come to die.
Let me drain the latest sup,
Shout Hurrah !—and then —good-bye.

CUI BONO?

WHEN the rose of a day is faded,
  And the dream of a month is o'er,
And the queen of an hour degraded
  To the place that she held before;
When the sun is about his setting
  O'er the morn that seems scarce begun,
What is the use of fretting
  Now—when it all is done?
    For the rose was a queen of roses,
      And the dream was so dear awhile,
    And the light of the day that closes
      Sets over a royal smile.

When the glow of the gilded summer
  Is lost in the winter's white ;
When the swallow—the faithless comer !—
  Is flown to a new delight;

When the tears of the rain are wetting
    The threads that the spinner spun,
What is the use of fretting
    Now—when it all is done?
      For the summer was fair in flying,
        And the birds were so gay o'erhead,
      And many the victims dying
        In the mesh that the spider spread.

When the lips are too sad for kisses,
    And the sight of the eyes is dimmed,
When the hearing is dulled and misses
    The sounds that were sweetly hymned;
When the days are beyond regretting
    And the sands in the glass are run,
What is the use of fretting
    Now—when it all is done?
      For the kisses were sweet in tasting
        And the chords were so full and deep!
      But the oil in the lamp is wasting,
        And now is the time for sleep.

SWALLOWS

———-

Down in the chasm below me you flutter, O swallow,
  Fearless and free.
Winged and unfettered as you, is my soul fain to follow
Out of the chasm and darkness, and up through the hollow
On to the downs where the wind bloweth fresh from the sea.
  Shall it not be ?

Here on the downs—where the murmurous voice of the
  ocean
  Rises and falls,
Lapping and laving in restless perpetual motion,
Kissing the feet of the cliffs with a tireless devotion,
Cliffs that rise up from it proudly, impregnable walls,
  Victors—not thralls.

Down in the bay see the shadow lies dark and enthralling,
     Sullen and grey.
But, where the uttermost crag throws its shadow appalling,
Cutting it through, lo, a pathway of glory is falling
Straight from the low-lying sun, at the Gates of the
    Day
      Passing away.

Glory that touches the shore where the darkness so present
     Deepest must be;
Over a tremulous ocean of hues evanescent
Leading away and away to a sky opalescent,
Distant and dim as a dream, fading into the sea.
     Whither ?—ah me !

Had I but wings as thou hast them, O swallow that fleeteth,
     Then would I fly !
Fly where the uttermost end of the glory-line meeteth
Close to the edge of the shore, in the land where none
    weeteth,
There where the sea melts to one with the hues of the
    sky.
     Is that—to die ?

Wings are within us, ah sure ! They are clipped, but
    their fretting
        Vexes us sore,
Beating by day and at night-time, and never forgetting
Freedom they knew, and a restlessness ever begetting
Fraught with a longing to break through all trammels
    and soar
        Free evermore.

MY KING

I WRAPPED my king in purple robe,
    I placed a crown upon his head;
His hands with sceptre and with globe
    I filled; before his feet I spread
All riches that a king should own,
And raised him on a golden throne.

I said :—My king is good and wise,
    And chivalrous, and strong and great;
I decked his mind in such a guise
    As appertains to kingly state.
Afar and near fair things I sought,
And gave unto him all I brought.

I did it all.   I cannot blame
    Him that he was not kingly born,
And that he had no natural claim
    To virtues that a king adorn.
Ah! no; he made no vain pretence;
'Twas I who lacked in common-sense.

But what I suffered when I found
    My king 'as other men '—none knows
Save I.   Then life seemed all unsound
    And sad, till patient Love arose
And showed me with a tender hand
Those things I failed to understand.

And then I saw with clearer eyes
    The joy that still remained to me,
And learned to justly love and prize
    The good that lives in him.   So he
Is still my king enthroned, whom I
Shall love and honour till I die.

JUST FOR AWHILE

O To be far beyond all seeing and hearing,
  Where endless peace and unknown quiet beguile
The heart from the unseen anguish of hoping and fearing.
  O for rest for awhile ! for rest for awhile !

Just to be safe beyond all standing and falling,
  Where right and wrong are as one, good things as vile!
Beyond all being, all doing and all recalling.
  O for rest for awhile ! for rest for awhile !

Just to be still—so still that there is no moving :
  Never the gasp of a sob to be hid in a smile.
Out of the fear of hating, the love of loving,
  O for rest for awhile ! for rest for awhile !

Just to be hushed so well that there is no waking.
  Beyond 'good-bye,' and the dread of the Dark Defile;
Beyond forgetting, forgiving, misjudging, mistaking,
  O for rest for awhile ! for rest for awhile.

TRANSFORMATIONS

Love came and sighed across my heart
  Soft as a murmur scarcely heard,
  And lo! its inmost depths were stirred;
And little joys, like crystal streams
  O'er arid wastes that drought has bared,
    Went trickling through its dreams.

Love came and breathed across my heart
  Warm as a balmy breath of spring,
  And straight it fell to blossoming;
And little buds began to start
  Where hitherto not anything
    Of life or joy had part.

Love came and dwelt within my heart
  Where all the scented blossoms spread
  A delicate and dainty bed;
With twining craft they swiftly crept
  And clustering round his golden head
    So bound him where he slept.

GOLDILOCKS

Ou! you winsome little fairy, Goldilocks!
Oh! you dancing, light and airy Goldilocks!
  With your eyes that shine so brightly,
  Little feet that trip so lightly,
  And your ways so gay and sprightly,
        Goldilocks!

Oh! your mouth is like a cherry, Goldilocks,
Set in dimples sweet and merry, Goldilocks:
  And your peals of happy laughter
  Leave a cheerful echo after
  As they ring from every rafter,
        Goldilocks.

Yes, you really are perfection, Goldilocks,

And a cure for all dejection, Goldilocks,

  With your speeches quaint and funny,

  And your kisses sweet as honey,

  And your little face so sunny,

    Goldilocks.

Life to you is very pleasant, Goldilocks,

For you live but in the Present, Goldilocks,

  And you never stoop to borrow

  Any thought of care or sorrow

  From the coming of to-morrow,

    Goldilocks.

BABY VISIONS

What are you thinking of, baby of mine?
　　　　What did you see
Made your lips smile and your pretty eyes shine?
　　　　Tell it to me.
Was it some queer little elfin whose face
　　　　Thus made you smile?
Did he stand making some funny grimace
　　　　At you the while?

Was it some dear little fairy who sings
　　　　Only to you,
Flutt'ring around you on butterfly wings
　　　　Golden and blue?

Was it some mem'ry of playmates you knew
   Ere you came here,
Sweet little spirits of babies like you
   Tiny and dear?

Was it an angel come down from above
   Stately and fair,
Watching my baby with eyes full of love,
   Breathing a prayer?
Ah! little baby, you're smiling again!
   What do you see?
Why are the visions to baby-sight plain
   Hidden from me?

A PERFECT DREAM

Sing to me now, my dear, a low sweet song,
And I will lie and dream
A dream that shall be also sweet, and long,
For it shall have for theme
You—only you.

Nay, not you all alone, for were it so
You surely would be sad
To be so lonely; thus my dream shall know
One more to make you glad,
You—and me too.

And so, being glad, and sweet beyond all thought,
And leaving time behind,
My dream shall be perfection, lacking naught,
A chain of gold entwined
Round me and you.

LOVE'S LANGUAGES

Though lips be mute and words be never spoken
   Sure little Love has myriad means whereby
He can with voiceless language plain betoken
        That he is nigh,
        Though lips be mute.

If eyes can speak, ah ! surely mine must tell you
   The love that thrills my being through and through,
And with soft pleadings, passion-fraught, compel you
        To love me too;
        If eyes can speak.

If touch say aught, my silent hand caressing
   Will speak a subtle language of its own,
A thousand tender messages addressing
        To you alone;
        If touch say aught.

Words are too poor !   The voice's soft inflections
  Suffice not all my heart would say to you;
Love's many tongues with all their sweet perfections
      Were yet too few !
    Words are too poor.

AUBADE

Awake, O world, my lady comes!
    My lady comes this way.
Her eyelids hide the light of stars
    Beneath their shrouding sway;
Her lips are like two coral bars
       That guard a strand
       Whose gleaming sand
    Is pearls in rich array.

Awake, O world, my lady comes!
    My lady comes this way.
Her hair is spun of stolen light
    From many a golden ray

Through woodland shadows falling bright;
       So every thread
       That decks her head
Is sunlight gone astray.

Awake, O world, my lady comes!
       My lady comes this way.
Her face is like an orchard-close
       When all abloom in May;
So deftly spread the white and red,
       That where they blend
       And where they end
No eye can surely say.

Awake, O world, my lady comes!
       My lady comes this way.
As stormy clouds or changing seas
       Her eyes are nameless grey,
And varying are their hues as these;
       And lightnings flash
       Beneath her lash,
Or sudden sunbeams play.

Awake, O world, my lady comes !
    My lady comes this way.
Let merle and throstle chaunt and fill
    The welkin with their lay,
Yet shall their sweetest music still
        Be dull and sad
        Against the glad
    Soft words that she will say.

Awake, O world, my lady comes !
    My lady comes this way.
The distant music of her feet,
    As fairy marches gay,
Comes swiftly, and with rustling fleet
        Her silken gown
        As falling down
    Of fountains' silvery spray.

SERENADE

Hush, O night, into silence, for fear
That you waken my dear,
For she lies
With the sound of her sleeping like sighs
When the soft zephyr blows
O'er the lips of a rose.

On the track of an arrogant star
As it falleth afar,
Out of Space
Come, O Dream, with its light on thy face;
On her fair pillow rest,
That her sleep may be blest.

And, O Dream, as thou waitest awhile
In the spell of her smile,
Prithee say
But my name at her ear, that it may
In a soft murmur slip
From the door of her lip.

THE YEAR'S FLITTING

A FLASH of the wind on the water
  That shatters to silver the grey;
A rush and a moan in the forest,
  And leaves that whirl madly away;
Then silence o'er water and woodland,
  And odours of damp and decay.

The ' mast ' of the beeches is lying
  So thick on the ground that we tread
The sound of our footfall is muffled
  Like footsteps that follow the dead;
And hark! through the copse goes a rustle
  —A spirit that shivered and fled.

The leaves of the bramble are spotted
With splashes of ruby, like gore;
Ah! yes, o'er their leafage is sprinkled
The blood of the year that is o'er
Whose ghost as it fled through the copses
Has bid us adieu evermore.

No wonder our hearts are so heavy,
And laughter is silenced in pain;
—The tears we let fall on a coffin,
Though swiftly as torrents of rain
They drip, with a pitiful patter,
Will wake not the sleeper again.

FROM THE SEA WALL

THE air was filled with wild tumultuous sound;
  The rush of many waters, and the crash
Of breaking waves; the madness of rebound
  When one returning met with furious clash
His swift oncoming brother, and they twain
Rose, in one mighty spray to fall again.

Yet dark and darker grew the angry night :
  But evermore along the curved sea-wall
Rose gleaming sprays, unearthly grand and white,
  That flashed and vanished. Then—most strange of all—
A round red moon, veiled weird and mistily,
  Leapt up in gloomy splendour from the sea.

But, climbing soon beyond the vapoury veil
  In red magnificence, across the wan
Wild waves she threw a flickering fiery trail
  That o'er the troubled surface fitful shone;
Then paling ever as she reached her height,
  She filled with floods of silver all the night.

II

R I V E R-S O N G

YE dear and dreamy autumn eves!
  In mellow light of closing day
  The river sings, and flows away
Flecked here and there with gilded leaves
That fall from golden trees who throw
Their imaged glory down below.

(Sing, river, sing, with silvern tongue
The song you sang when all was young).

The swallows, that a week ago
  Were swiftly darting here and there,
  Are gone; and all the evening air

Is noisy with the homing crow;
While far away the mill-wheel's drone
Makes solemn music of its own.

(Sing, river, sing, the song you've sung
Since I and all the world were young).

The robin's wintry voice is heard
 At vespers in the neighbouring tree;
 The noiseless gnats dance lazily;
And now and then the pool is stirred
To circles widening ring on ring
By some late troutlet's sudden spring.

(Sing, river, sing as you have sung
Ere life's dead leaves were o'er you flung).

The clouds hang motionless on high;
 There's not a breath to stir the leaves;
 And soft and slowly evening weaves
The veil that shrouds all days that die.
The sounds grow silent one by one,
Alone the river ne'er has done.

(Sing, river, sing. Your song is sung
Though life or love be old or young).

VER VARIABLE

MARCH 9TH. MORNING.

———

I HAVE seen her!   She is here!
    She is with us once again!
    In her kingdom come to reign,
Dainty queen of all the year.

And she touched me as she passed.
    Oh her touch was warm and sweet!
    I could hear her fairy feet
O'er the daisies flitting fast.

Swift I followed where she trod ;
    Glad I followed where she led.
    Every footstep as she fled
Called a blossom from the sod.

And I gathered as I went
    Growing sunshine—celandine,
    Growing sunshine—crocus sheen.
Oh my heart was well content.

Full of fragrance was the day,
    For the perfume of her mouth
    Is as when the balmy South
Wooes the violet-souls away.

Blue her eyes and very kind,
    Full of laughter and delight ;
    Doubly tender, doubly bright
From the tears that lurk behind.

Little primroses a-row,
    —Creamy yellow, pearly white,
    Or in rose or crimson dight—
Watched, with golden eyes aglow

As she tripped along the line.
    And the bees sang soft and low
    As they flitted to and fro
'Mid the snows of laurestine.

How the sunlight flashed and shone
     On the polished leaves that spread
     Every shade of green and red
That a berberis can don.

Then a blackbird whistled clear,
     And the thrushes were about ;
     While the sparrows—merry rout—
Chirped and gabbled 'Spring is here' !

And the starlings chattered fast
     'Spring is come, so let us build
     In the chimney that we filled
With our nests—as in the past.'

All is fresh, and fair, and dear,
     All is bright, and gay, and glad.
     Who could let himself be sad
When he knew the Spring is here ?

II

MARCH 9TH. EVENING.

Across the silence of the night
     The melancholy breezes sigh

A soft and sea-like melody
As down the vale they take their flight.

An owl cries sadly from the glen ;
The stars are hid ; the moon is pale
And sorrowing 'neath a vapoury veil.
The neighbouring clock strikes slowly 'ten.'

No footsteps wander here so late ;
No voice disturbs the silent lane.
The breezes sigh and sigh amain,
And it is lonely at the gate.

III

MARCH 10TH. MORNING.

RAIN, rain, rain, rain.
Spring is fled away again.

Whither, whither is she fled
From the sullen grey o'erhead ?

Hath no mortal eye descried
Where our lovely Spring doth hide ?

Hath she left us in disdain,
Or will she return again?

Is she hiding but awhile
That we pine to see her smile?

Will she break on us anon
When we deem her wholly gone?

From her nook steal out with glee,
Laughing merrily to see

That our foolish eyes are wet
With impatience and regret?

Yes, I know she is at play.
In her haste to hide away

She hath left so many signs
That betray her sly designs;

She forgot to shut the eyes
Of the daisies—oh unwise!—

She forgot to nip the shoots
Springing up from hidden roots ;

She forgot to still in death
All the violets' gentle breath;

And so hurried was her flight
She forgot the primrose quite !

Then she never hushed the birds,
Who with sympathetic words

Minister to our despair,
Saying :—' Joy is everywhere,

' For though hidden is our Queen
She was with us yester-e'en.

· When she ran away to hide
We flew softly by her side,

' So we know her lurking-place ;
And we see her smiling face

' Peeping out with arch delight.
    Cheer you, mortal sad, despite

' That it rain, and rain and rain ;
    Spring will soon look forth again ! '

    Let us catch the gay refrain :—
' Though it rain, and rain and rain,
    Spring will soon look forth again ! '

'\WHO ARE YOU?'

(An old print of a little child and a little Faun meeting)

———

WHEN the world was in its childhood
  And the gods were known of men ;
When the meadow and the wild wood
  Had its special denizen;
When the half-man and the true man
  Dwelt beneath the arching blue,
Little Faun and little human
  Laughing questioned—'Who are you?'

Laughing questioned—laughed replying,
  Unamazed and undismayed;
Neither from the other flying,
  On the sward together played.

So the Spirits of the meadows,
   Founts and woodlands, free and wild,
And the living lights and shadows
   Were the playmates of the child.

Then he watched the Naiad sleeping
   Where the whisp'ring waters fell ;
With the light-foot Faun went leaping
   Gay and gladly through the dell;
Chased the shy-eyed Oread flying
   Swiftly over hill and lea;
Wept the Hamadryad dying
   Slowly in her dying tree.

Then the love of lovely faces
   Watched him through the woodland dim;
And the quiet country places
   Friendly greetings held for him.
So to friendship closely growing
   Perfect sympathy began,
And the love from Nature flowing
   Echoed in the soul of man.

Fauns are dead !—At least they say so,
  People who are old and wise—
Naiads too ! Ah well, it may so
  Be; I look with other eyes.
Come with me. They are but hiding;
  Naiads sing beside the rill;
Fauns in field and wood are 'biding.
  Trust me, they are living still.

Come with me. The world is teeming
  With the living thoughts of old,
Only we have lost their seeming
  'Mid life's movement manifold.
Let us leave the pain and riot,
  Leave the busy haunts of men,
And in Nature's peopled quiet
  We will both grow young again.

IN THE CLOUDS

I saw the sun look o'er a bank of grey ;
   He fringed its edges with a silver fringe,
   And o'er the sky below it threw a tinge
Like apricots that on a southern wall
Grow mellow to their richest in his ray.

I saw a prophet in the clouds to-day,
   A mighty man, severe, and hoar with eld;
   One upward hand in admonition held;
He seemed instinct with wrath and prophecy
And voiceless warning to the sons of clay.

I saw a woman;—still and wondrous fair
   She leaned upon the battlements on high,
   And dreamed across the hollow arch of sky;
And all her soul seemed gazing in her eyes.
Then soft she melted in the ambient air.

IN THE WOODS IN SPRING

OVERHEAD the fairy fretwork
  Of the larchen boughs was hung,
Like a brown enamel network,
  All with emerald glories strung.

Little sunbeam-children playing
  In the arching branches, strewed
Little golden rags and tatters,
  On the carpet of the wood.

And the carpet of the woodland
  Was of pattern choice and rare,
Trails of ivy for a back-ground,
  With a dead leaf here and there.

Over this the flowers were scattered,
    Just as Spring had thrown them down
When she passed with myriad blossoms,
    Carried in her dainty gown.

Running by, a wealthy streamlet
    Who some rich Golconda owns,
Was with lavish hand bestrewing
    Rainbow gems o'er moss and stones.

And the birds were singing gaily;
    They had many things to say
What with making love and talking
    To their neighbours all the day.

' Have you found a place for building ? '
    ' Tell me when your nest is done ! '
' How are Mrs Robin's children ?
    My poor wife has only one.'

' Mrs Sparrow's had the Cuckoo
    Calling at her house again ! '
' Mr Chaffinch has got married ;
    She, poor thing, is very plain ! '

'Do you love me, love me, love me ? '
　'Yes, I love you, very dear ! '
So the birds are singing gaily,
　In the Springtime of the year.

And the Woodpecker, the cynic,
　With his little fez of red,
Spends his time in loudly laughing
　At the things that they have said.

MISNOMERS

WHEN erst the sunlight breaks the mould
In tiny cups of glittering gold
    Upheld on dainty trays of green,
    —Fit goblet for the Fairy Queen—
We mortals hail them with delight,
And call the sweet things ' Aconite.'

And when the silver bells—that swing
On slender ropes of green to ring
    The advent of the fairy train
    That comes the golden cups to drain
Are white upon the grass, we say :—
' The snowdrops all are out to-day ! '

How blind, alas! poor mortals be,
Who fail the fairy folk to see,
    And do not know when they behold,
    The banquet spread with cups of gold,
Or hear the merry chime that swells
From such a host of silver bells.

EVENING

THE sky is all hooded and shrouded with grey,
 The night stealeth rapidly on,
But one little cloud that belonged to the day
 Refuses to fade and begone.
It drifts o'er the shadows, a delicate sprite
In gossamer garments of apricot light,
And bids a delicious defiance to night.

Athwart all the shadows one tremulous ray
 Of sunlight hath sought it, and shone
In sweet benediction, all golden and gay,
 For that little cloudlet alone.
It climbs, as I watch it, that ladder of light,
And out through the greyness it passes from sight.
Who'll follow? who'll follow? I would if I might.

ON THE MOOR

———.

I *cannot* read. 'Tis useless quite.
   I needs must look and listen ;
Must watch the changing western light ;
   Must see the water glisten,
And hear the music that it makes
   When rushing o'er the pebbles,
And list the passing breeze that wakes
   The slender grassy trebles.

Dear world of details !—far too fine
   For any words to tell them.
This lumbering tongue and pen of mine
   In vain essay to spell them.

'Tis but the soul of every sense
  That comprehends them thoroughly,
And filled with wondering reverence
  Can estimate them truly.

There is so much to hear and see,
  So little time to do it.
O let me grasp what hours there be
  Lest losing I should rue it.
I'll keep the black and white for days
  Whose spells are not so binding.
—But when, 'mid Nature's varied ways
  Can I pretend the finding?

WIND SONG

Blow, wind!   Blow as you will:
  Shout and whistle by scaur and fell ;
Wake the world with your piping shrill ;
  Hoot and hurry by hill and dell.

Blow, wind!   Blow as you will,
My heart's best love is my heart's love still.

Blow wind!   Blow as you list ;
  Toss and tumble the waves at sea ;
Clear the day from its cloak of mist ;
  Lilt of laughter and lightsome glee.

Blow, wind!   Blow as you will.
My heart's best love is my heart's love still.

Blow, wind! Blow as you will;
  Moan and mutter the trees among;
Sing of spring to the world, and fill
  Hearts with hopes that are fair and young.

Blow, wind! Blow as you will,
My heart's best love is my heart's love still.

Blow, wind! Blow as you list!
  Sigh and tremble along the grass;
Buds will break that your lips have kissed,
  Break and blossom to see you pass.

Blow, wind! Blow as you will,
My heart's best love is my heart's love still.

THE SUN'S WOOING

THE grey dawn stood in quiet mood,
    The merry Sun crept up behind her,
And laughing o'er her shoulder, strove
    With sudden blaze of light to blind her.
She turned, and gazing in his face,
    She lost herself in his embrace.

EARTH'S MUSIC

Lie prone upon the moor to hear
  The music that the world is making.
The heather bells ring shrill and clear
  When passing breezes set them shaking.

The slender pipes of yellow grass,
  Flute tiny music, soft and mellow,
As water when the ripples pass
  Each madly racing with his fellow.

The runnel gurgles round the stones;
  It has three voices in its singing,
Here solemn bass—here tenor tones,—
  And there a treble clear and ringing.

The bees go humming in and out

   The scented bloom of gorse and heather,

And gay cicalas hop about,

   And chirrup of the sunny weather.

And thousand, thousand other sounds,

   Indefinite, but sweet and cheering,

All swell the music that abounds

   About our path and needs but hearing.

THE 'WAGGONER'S WELL'

THERE's a track that leads over the common,
  Where the gorse and the heather are rank,
Then it dips down a lane thro' the copses,
  With mosses and ferns on the bank;
And deep through the woodland declining,
  It slopes to the foot of the dell,
Where it widens away to a level,
  Close down by the ' Waggoner's Well.'
      Oh ! hark to the waggoner's whistle,
        And the crack of his whip in the dell;
      His horses are always so eager
        To drink at the ' Waggoner's Well.'

He's a face that is honest and ruddy,
  He has eyes of the cheeriest blue;
And his heart is as light as a feather,
  His whistle is mellow and true.

The girls in the village all know him:
Scarce one from the other he'll tell,
But there's Someone he knows in a cottage,
    That's near to the 'Waggoner's Well.'
        Oh ! hark to the waggoner's whistle,
            And the crack of his whip in the dell;
            His horses are always so willing
            To loiter at ' Waggoner's Well.'

When the crack of the whip and the whistle
    Are heard in the woodland's repose,
There's a flash as of fluttering raiment,
    A vision with cheeks like a rose,
And lips that are rosy and pouting;
    No doubt that they muttered a spell,
For the waggoner stands in a moment
    Transfixed by the 'Waggoner's Well.'
        And hushed is the waggoner's whistle,
            But why ? Do not ask me to tell.
            His horses have time to grow weary
            Of waiting at ' Waggoner's Well.'

WISHES

Oh leaves that float, and fade, and die,
  Adown the whirling stream,
Then sing to rest within its breast,
  And sleep and do not dream.
So would I sleep when restless day
Melts into shadowy night away.

Oh birds that wake, and chirp, and sing
  A cheerful matin tune,
To find each day more fair and gay
  As May climbs into June.
So would I wake when night is o'er
To find day fairer than before.

MY CLOUD

THE clouds are hanging low to-day ;
    So low it almost seems if I
    But stretched my eager arms on high
    That I might grasp a snowy cloud,
    And wrap it round me as a shroud,
And thus enfolded pass away.

Away, away, o'er hills and dales ;
    Above the river's silver line,
    Above the drowsy feeding kine ;
    Above the cities of the dead
    Who lie so lowly, stone at head,
To wait until the trumpet hails.

Away, away, on wings of air !

    O'er pastures lying broad and green ;

    O'er shimmering cornfields' golden sheen,

    Where stalwart reapers working stand

    With sickles flashing in their hand,

With sunbrowned arms and throat all bare.

Away, away, across the sea ;

    Above the little fishing town,

    And past the flying sails of brown.

    My cloud and I have downward cast

    A purple shadow as we passed

O'er ocean's bosom airily.

Away, away, so high and free !

    Below—the tree-tops green and high ;

    Above—the endless arch of sky.

    And just one little lark up there,

    A living song that seems to share

The welkin with my cloud and me.

Away, away, so fleet we go !

    Across the moorland lone and wide ;

    O'er hills in wealthiest purple dyed ;

O'er red-roofed cots with eyes of fire,

O'er glitt'ring roof and gilted spire :

The vesper bell rings faint below.

And westering with the parting sun

    We float into an amber sea ;

    And my sweet cloud, it seems to me,

    Has wings of gold and crimson hue,

    And strange deep eyes of starlight blue ;

    In tender arms he doth me hold,

    And bears me on through gates of gold,

And this is heaven—and life's begun !

THE RIVER

SEE the lights upon the river !
    They are broad and clear and bright,
And they sweep across its current
    With a still and lovely light,
Tracing out its distant passage
    Where it else would cheat the eye,
Breaking up its darkest shadows
    With a message from the sky.

The reflections on the river,
    They are fresh and true and fair;
Every leaf that hangs above it
    Finds his fellow leaflet there;

K

The eternal hills stand on it,
   And the cloudlets drift along;
Yet beneath the painted surface
   Flows the river full and strong.

And the shadows of the river,
   They are rich and strong and deep;
Colour-notes of fullest music
   That in chords harmonious sweep;
There is no unbroken *blackness*
   Where the darkened waters run;
It is only deeper colour
   Waiting for a glint of sun.

O the ripples of the river,
   How they dance and laugh and sing,
Making merry in the shallows,
   Seeking joy in everything.
How they leap across the pebbles
   That are strewn along the way,
Finding in the worst obstruction
   Only reason to be gay.

And the currents of the river,
 Where they deep and stately glide
With a strong still onward movement
 That for nothing turns aside.
No small troubles jar and fret them,
 But with firm resistless force,
Undelaying and unstaying
 They go forward on their course.

Oh my heart be like the river!
 Let the lights of heaven shine
On your way, and sweet reflections
 Fill your paths with hues divine.
Be your shadows full of colour;
 Life and sweet content agree;
And your course be strong and steadfast
 Till at length you reach the sea.

THE WITCHES' FROLIC

How happy is the Witch
When night is dark as pitch
And clouds are scudding madly o'er the sky;
She takes her little broom
And mounting through the gloom,
'Mid all the rack and tumult she will fly.

Hurrah ! hurrah ! for the wind is fierce and loud !
Hurrah ! hurrah ! for the night is black as pitch !
Hurrah ! hurrah ! for we are a jovial crowd,
And the Brocken is the haven of the witch !

For all the bygone week
She has been so still and meek,
So gentle and so quiet and so good,
That no one ever dreamed
She was not all she seemed,
—But now she mounts her little steed of wood.

Hurrah! hurrah! for the brooms are all in flight!
Hurrah! hurrah! for the sky is black as pitch!
Hurrah! hurrah! we shall have a jolly night
For the Brocken is the haven of the witch!

The thunders roar and crash,
The lightnings flare and flash,
The witches dance and revel, shriek and squall;
And looking quite sublime,
With one hoof beating time
'Old Clootie' stands and smiles upon them all.

Hurrah! hurrah! for the lightning flickers blue!
Hurrah! hurrah! for the skies are black as pitch!
Hurrah! hurrah! for we are a merry crew,
And the Brocken is the haven of the witch!

WINTER'S WATCHMAN

LIKE a watchman on the housetop
   Who awaits the break of morning,
And from off his lofty standpoint
   Looks across the twilight hush,
To awake the silent sleepers
   With a joyful shout of warning,
When the sunrays fill the greyness
   With a warm and vivid flush.

So the wakeful woodbine clambers
   From the place where all is sleeping,
In the twilight hush of Winter,
   When the days are dark and drear,

And a patient watch, unwearied,
   From his point of vantage keeping,
Is the first to fill the copses
   With the cry that Spring is near.

See his tufts of tender verdure,
   How they break the solemn dulness
That the hues of winter carry,
   With a shaft of summer's light;
How they fill the empty hedges
   With a sense of coming fulness,
And remind the world of morning,
   When it only dreamed of night.

THE SPRING GOES BY !

DANCE little streamlets, laughing o'er the lea;
Dance with the gladsomeness of Spring-tide glee.
 Sing, little songsters, loud and clear and long;
 Sing with the sweetness of a Spring-tide song.
Sail, little clouds, across an azure sky;
Sail swift to see her, for the Spring goes by.

Laugh, little breezes, breathing loud or low;
Laugh near the rootlets; bid the blossoms blow.
 Bloom, little flowers, that by your fragrant scent
 All men may know the way her footsteps went.
Shine, golden sun ! Make light that all may spy
How fair the world is when the Spring goes by.

Wave, rustling branches, in the balmy air,
Wreathe emerald glories in your dark brown hair;
 Don, dainty larches, rosy rubies too;
 Spring is the fairest time of all for you.
Let all glad things to join the pageant hie.
Make haste, make haste, O world ! The Spring goes by !

AT ONE

ALONE upon the moor.   The darkness grows,
  And soon the night will hide the world away.
We are at one, dark hour; my spirit knows
  All these thy parts and signs :—the climbing grey
And ragged clouds that veil the rose and blue
  Of upper heaven; the constant silver star
That waits a rifting cloud, and shineth through;
  The chilly wind that cometh from afar,
With tears and sighing laden, but that makes
  Its sorrow into music 'mong the reeds,
And fills the silence with a song that takes
  Its sweetness from the sadness where it breeds;
The cheery lights that burn with steadfast glow,
  To mark the warmth of other people's fires,

Too far away for night and me to know

    Their joys and sorrows, or their hearts' desires;

And out beyond the loneness of the moor,

    The sounds that rise of stirring outer life,

So far from us that scarcely are we sure

    The same world holds us that is *there* so rife

With noise of barking dogs and rolling wheels,

    And *here* so filled with solitary peace,

—That sad glad loneliness that heartward steals,

    And while we sigh bids all our sorrow cease.

ROSES

THERE is a time when the roses bloom
  Sweet and fair;
  And the warm noon air
Sates itself with the rich perfume,
And the night-wind sighs through the scented gloom.
Sweet is the time when the roses bloom.

There is a time when the roses fade.
  Fresh were they,
  But the fervid day
Fainted them, and they mourned for shade,
Each sweet rose at her heart afraid.
Sad is the time when the roses fade.

There is a time when the roses die,—
  Nothing left
  But a stem bereft;
Petals sere on the brown earth lie;
Night winds mourn as they pass thereby.
Woe is the time when the roses die.

THE YEAR'S MISERS

GOLDEN leaves that hold so closely
  All the sunshine of the year,
At your falling it will vanish
  Till in Spring ye re-appear.
All your treasure take ye with you !
  All your greedy hands can hold !
Stolen wealth of dewdrop jewels;
  Heapéd gain of sunlight gold.

But no misers ye in spending
  All your hidden hoarded store.
When the earth is bare and sorry,
  When the flowers are seen no more,

Ye are spending, spending, spending,
  Shut in silence, out of sight;
And the left hand of your giving
  Has no knowledge of the right.

All the glitter of your fortune
  Passes from you; what ye stole
From the summer you have hoarded
  That ye may return the whole.
Not alone just as you had it,
  —That were poor and vain to tell—
But with interest over-measured,
  For ye give yourselves as well.

So when Spring's first sunshine quivers
  Over branches golden-green
We shall read the tender story
  Of the leaves that once have been.
We shall see that silent effort
  Spreads its influence far and wide,
And that earth is brighter, better,
  For the lives of leaves that died.

WHAT SHALL WE BE?

Say—shall we be two roses on one tree
    To bud and bloom in the same sunny weather,
To welcome to our hearts the same brown bee,
    In the same wind to bend and bow together?
Called by the same dear fragrant name of rose,
    Watched by the same clear stars above us beaming;
Kissed by the same soft Zephyr, as it goes;
    Lulled by the same sweet nightingale to dreaming.
Then, when the days of bloom are over-past,
    And fading-time is come and time for dying,
Shed earthward in the same wild gale at last,
    And on the same kind mould together lying?

Say—shall we be two little streams that flow
    Through the same meadow all with flowers enamelled;
Making the same clear music as we go
    Down to the river on our course untrammelled?

By the same rain-rush brimming full and high;

   The same blue sky and floating clouds reflecting;

Seeing the birds above us skim and fly;

   By the same slope our onward way directing?

Leaving the flowery meadows, side by side,

   And flowing swiftly down the grassy dingle;

Rushing together to the river's tide,

   In its embrace to meet and intermingle?

Say—shall we be two snowy clouds that fleet

   Across an azure sky in sunny hours,

Fanned by one breeze, and lying at our feet

   One wild wide moor, all gay with purple flowers?

Hearing the same sweet lark that soars and sings;

   On the same course by one swift impulse going;

Brushing the same great hill with fleecy wings,

   The same soft shadows on the moorland throwing?

Drawn at the last by some resistless power

   Our filmy folds towards each other urging;

Meeting, and in one rainbow-smitten shower

   Our parted lives in one existence merging.

FATALITY

O FATAL eyes !
I looked into their endless depths and saw
  The lurking Lurline softly, slowly rise,
With beckoning, gleaming arms, outstretched to draw
  Me down—down—down; and deep in their embrace
  My soul now drownèd lies.

O fatal eyes !
I gazed across the cold grey world and met
  A glorious blaze of all-transcendent light
That dimmed the fairest suns that rise and set,
  And blotted out Past, Present and To Be,
  —And leaves me blinded quite.

O fatal eyes!

Gates of the Paradise of dreams and spells,

Wide stood ye, and I entered wistfully

To find the Heart of Mystery that dwells

Therein.   And now the gates are closed for aye

Betwixt the world and me.

O fatal eyes!

Strange bourne from which no soul alive returns!

Where fair mirages paint a desert land

With unfulfilled delights; the hot sun burns,

And the lorn traveller perishes amid

The whirlwind and the sand.

PILGRIMAGE

WHITHER away?
Across the moorland brown and dim
' Beyond the utmost purple rim,'
　　Close in the wake of the wandering day,
To find the distant isles that lie
Purple and gold, and with shores of fire
　　In the still pale green of a waveless sea;
For surely there is my heart's desire
　　Which the earth has hidden away from me.
　　　I will search the sky.

　　Whither away?
Across the darkness that hath wed
The sleeping land, until I tread
　　Out on the waters that wash the bay,
Just where the clear moon's silvery track
Touches the shore, like a path that trends
　　To a far-off country that no one knows;
For surely there, where the pathway ends,
　　I shall find my lost, and my heart's repose,
　　　And never come back.

'FEET OF CLAY'

Our dearest idol has but feet of clay.
We know it, so why rudely rend away
   The robes that wrap them softly, and disguise;
Nay, rather let us looking upward, say :—
   'I see thy godhead shining in thine eyes.'

Thus, holding up our best unto its best,
Owning that only—though we know the rest,
   Conscious that we too stand on earthy feet,
We find that dual nature doubly blest,
   Rendering our idol to our needs complete.

For were our god all-perfect, we should be
So over-awed by its divinity,
   So crushed with our unequal littleness,
That we should lose its dear humanity,
   And Love would die for lack of a caress.

TO THE SEA

O SEA,—o'er whom one distant sail
Moves westward to the setting sun
The gathering cloud will soon prevail,
And o'er thy waters wide and dun
The mournful breezes wail.

Then all the gladness and delight
That lit thy ripples through the day
Wilt thou forget, and mad with fright
Wilt lash and dash in fierce dismay
Against the growing night.

And thou wilt stir the idle sand
Where once thy wavelets lapped the gold,
Befouling with a senseless hand
Thine own translucence; from its hold
Throw seaweed on the strand.

And thou wilt break thy perfect flow
  To shivered atoms on the rocks,
In vain attempt to overthrow
  By violence and sudden shocks
    That which the ages know.

Have done! have done! When morning breaks
  Across thy troubled waves once more,
Thou'lt see too late, with heart that aches,
  The mass of wreckage on the shore
    That lawless passion makes.

DAYS' DEATHS

———

I

On lovely winter eve! The leas
   Lie wan and whitely wrapped in snow.
The distant hedges and the trees
   Stand black against the western glow.
The moon-boat sails serenely through
The purple sea o'erhead, and two
   Or three bright stars look down to see
   How fair a winter's eve can be.

II

The ending of another day.
   Soft fleecy tender greys o'erhead,
A west of broken gold and grey,
   Touched lightly here and there with red.

A sleepy mill-wheel's lazy whirr,
  The murmur of the flowing leat,
Bird-twitters making everywhere
  A vesper service clear and sweet.
A swift keen winter wind that soughs
And troubles in the leafless boughs.

Later—a Sky-scape.

A lake of gold with rosy flushes;
A strand of pearl with sunset blushes;
  Low rocks of grey, 'mid roseate sedges;
  Grey hills behind with fiery edges.

III

A foreground dim and undefined;
A range of purple hills behind;
  Bare trees writ black and clear and high,
  Against a deepening orange sky.
A long low cloud of purplish grey,
That cuts the mellow light away
  From where it softly tones its hue
  To where it grows a turquoise blue.
Above—grey clouds whose fringes low
Reflect the warmth of western glow.

IV

A glorious globe of burning gold,
  Like some great lamp defined and clear,
That toward the dim and distant wold
  Sinks slowly, soon to disappear.
Across the golden glowing face,
In pencilling delicate as lace,
A poplar's leafless branches trace
  Their outline.   Through the atmosphere
The glow grows greater as it sinks;
  The upper clouds reflect the light,
And all the arching heaven drinks
  Deep draughts of roseate delight.
The range its lower circle clips !
It slowly, slowly, deeper dips !
At last behind the hill it slips !
  Good-night, O lamp of heaven, good-night !

MOON-RAYS

I

A SILVER mist on shining wings;
   A filmy mist that veils the moon
   And hides her beauty over-soon.
A mystic haze that sways and swings
To unseen melody that flings
   Across the heavens an endless tune.

II

A stern dark cloud that veiled the moon.
   It swept with dusky wings unfurled
   And hid her fair face from the world;
So reft night of her dearest boon.
   How dark the cloud! But it was thus
   Because we saw its hither side.
   Could but the other be descried
How bright it were! How glorious!

IN SPRING

WHEN Spring's fair fingers touch the waiting world,
When ferny fronds are daintily unfurled,
  And hedgerows don their robes of tender green,
  While starry blossoms on their banks are seen,
Then the gay heart makes haste to laugh and sing
' How good it is to be alive in Spring! '

By river-paths, when tasselled willows sway,
And laughing breezes steal their scent away;
  When bending trees, unfolding summer's dress
Reflect on their approaching loveliness,
Then the gay heart makes haste to laugh and sing
' How good it is to be alive in Spring! '

On wind-swept commons, when the golden bloom
Fills all the air with delicate perfume,
  When rose-lipped daisies ope a golden eye
  And smile an answer to the smiling sky,
Then the gay heart makes haste to laugh and sing
' How good it is to be alive in Spring! '

NOTES IN A GARDEN

———

I

WHEN soughs the wind to tell of coming rain,
  And all the shivering leaves in haste upturn,
When creeping shadows sadden all the plain,
  And overhead the cloud hangs black and stern,
Th' aspiring hills, with golden crests unbowed,
Shine in the sun that burns above the cloud.

II

  The shower is over; and the cloud
    Has, rifting, left us breaks of blue
  Like open windows, with a crowd
    Of laughing sunbeams looking through.

It seems as though the world forgot
So soon her little hour of grief.
But listen—on the ivied cot
The tears slip down from leaf to leaf.

III

Flushed with the passion of the hills,
The river rushes fierce and red;
A thousand unsuspected rills
Its powerful stream have fed.

Swift in the ardour of its course,
All idle things it sweeps away,
And vanquishes with headlong force
The stronghold of decay.

Filled with a discontent divine,
The fairest meads it hurries by;
And only asks at even-shine,
In the great sea to die.

IV

The quiet moon like some lone maid
Walks whitely through the garish day,

And, till its gilded course is stayed,
    None marks her unobtrusive way.

But when the faithless sun is fled,
    She stands alone serene and bright,
And by her patient rays are led,
    Some errant footsteps home aright.

V

An owl cried out as the daylight passed
    O'er a sea of gold to the distant west;
While overhead, like a curtain vast
    To close the scene of the day's unrest,
A cloud of purple—whose folds were red
With the dying fire of the sun—was spread.

As I watched the glory that paled and waned,
    And the grey that crept where the flush had died,
The sense grew keen that the world was pained,
    And my heart cried out as the owl had cried.

VI

The moon dropped threads of silver through the night ;
    Then deftly weaving to a gleaming skein,
She threw the glittering thing across the plain,
    And lo !—a river flashing silver-white.

SCRAPS

To do the thing he should not do
Man yearns since the beginning.
To find a sin were not a sin
Would spoil the zest of sinning.

ONE saw a star reflected in a pool,
-A little muddy puddle by the road,-
And thought it was a real star, so tried
To grasp it, often; then the puddle dried,
And left no star at all! So off he strode
Disgusted, murmuring: 'I have been a fool!'

His life is best that memory shrines as good,
  And other praise than this it needeth not.
Then next to him in Death's close brotherhood
  His life is well that can be well forgot.

———

' ALL things will come '—so people say—
  ' To him who waits.'   In sooth
If he but wait perchance they may,
  Save one that comes no more for aye
But far and farther drifts away.
  That sweet lost good is Youth.

BY LOT

HERE let me set them side by side,
    These cups alike in all
Their outward seeming, but so wide
    In aught that must befall
The lips that drain them. This indeed
    Is pure, life-giving wine;
And that?—that holds for hearts that bleed
    A certain anodyne
Whereby forgetfulness will steal
    O'er all the bygone pain,
And power to hear and see and feel
    Will never wake again.
I set them here; so knowing not
    When night has hid them up
Which one is which, leave Fate the lot
    To deal the appointed cup.
My only part will be to drain
    The draught she gives, and wait
To sleep for aye, or wake again,
    To bless or curse my fate.

THE END